Enid Blyton's
SECRET TOYBOX TALES

ILLUSTRATED BY ROBIN LAWRIE

TEMPLAR

A TEMPLAR BOOK

Devised and produced by The Templar Company plc,
Pippbrook Mill, London Road, Dorking, Surrey RH4 IJE

This edition produced in the UK for Bookmart Ltd.

These stories were first published in Sunny Stories, Tiny Tales, Read To Us,
The Enid Blyton Pennant Series and Two Years in The Infant School 1926 to 1953
These poems were first published in various collections 1923 to 1968

Edited by Caroline Repchuk
Designed by Mark Kingsley-Monks

Printed and bound in Italy

ISBN 1-898784-44-2

CONTENTS

FUNNY THOUGHTS

I thought each day, when I was one,
That someone had to light the sun.

When I was two, I thought the moon
Was just a very big balloon.

When I was three, I thought the train
Went round the world and back again.

When I was four, I thought I might
Slip down the bath-hole any night.

I always thought, when I was five,
My toys and dolls would come alive.

I thought I saw, when I was six,
A fairy hiding in my bricks.

When I was seven, I felt sure
A giant lived behind our door.

When I was eight, I thought I'd be
A knight, and set princesses free.

What funny thoughts I had! Did you?
Do think of some and tell them, too!

TIT FOR TAT

Jennifer, the curly-haired doll, had a little hairbrush of her own. She was very proud of it indeed, and the toys liked it too, because it was fun to brush out Jennifer's lovely golden curls at night. Sometimes she lent it to the toys. Then the teddy bear brushed his short fur, the black dog brushed his mop of black hair, the pink cat brushed his coat and the clockwork mouse brushed his whiskers.

The little hairbrush lived in a small box. Sally, the little girl who owned all the toys, never bothered with it at all. She hadn't brushed Jennifer's hair once with it, so it was a good thing the toys took turns at brushing her hair to make it look nice.

Then one day a most annoying thing happened. Sally was cleaning out her dolls' house and she wanted a brush to sweep the little carpets. She didn't want to borrow Mummy's brush because it was much too big for the tiny carpets. So can you guess what she did? She borrowed Jennifer's little hairbrush. Just the thing!

"It's just right for this job," said Sally, brushing away at the carpet. "What a good thing I thought of it."

But the toys didn't think so at all! They looked on in dismay and Jennifer was almost in tears. Her own little hairbrush! How mean of Sally!

"Now I shan't be able to brush my hair with it any more," she thought. "It will be dirty and horrid. I do wish Sally had used something else. It's too bad of her."

Sally finished brushing the carpets and looked at the little brush. Such hard sweeping had almost worn it out. "It's no use now," she said. "I'll throw it away." And into the fire it went! Oh, dear! The toys watched it blaze into flames for a minute or two – and then it was gone!

Jennifer cried that night. "I did like my little hairbrush," she said. "I've got such a lot of hair that I need a brush for it. Sally never brushes it for me. She doesn't look as if she brushes her own hair, either."

"She's an untidy little girl," said the bear. "She doesn't brush her teeth either. But she tells her mother that she does. She's a naughty story-teller."

"Yes, she is," said the pink cat. "Her mother gave her a nice new green toothbrush last week and Sally hasn't used it yet! She hasn't cleaned her teeth all week."

"Then a toothbrush is just wasted on her!" said the clockwork mouse. "It's a pity we can't take it and use it to brush Jennifer's hair each night!"

"That's a very fine idea, Mouse!" said the bear. "However did you think of it?"

The clockwork mouse would have blushed with delight at this praise if he could. "I don't know how I thought of it," he said. "I must be cleverer than I imagined."

"Shall we get Sally's toothbrush then?" said the pink cat. "I could climb up to the basin in the bathroom and reach up for it, I think. It's in her mug."

"All right. You go then," said the bear, and the pink cat went. He was quite good at jumping. He leapt up to the basin, climbed up on to the shelf above, took Sally's perfectly new toothbrush in his mouth and jumped down to the floor again.

He padded into the playroom with it. The toys looked at it.

"The handle's too long," said the bear. "Much too long."

"Cut a bit off then," said the pink cat.

"Sally's got some tools in a box," said Jennifer, the doll. "There's a little saw there. We could use that."

They found the little saw, and the bear sawed away at the handle of the toothbrush. Everyone watched in excitement. The end of the handle suddenly fell off. The mouse picked up the little brush in delight. "Its handle is nice and short now," he said. "Just right for a hairbrush. Jennifer, do let me brush your hair for you."

So he was the first to brush the doll's curly hair with the new brush. It brushed beautifully because it had harder bristles than the hairbrush. Jennifer was delighted.

"Where shall we keep this brush?" asked the bear. "Better not put it into the box because Sally might see it."

"Put it into me," said the little tin teapot, in a spouty voice. "Sally never plays with me now. She'll never look inside me."

So that is where the toys keep the new hairbrush. The bear was a little bit worried at first. "Do you think we've done wrong to use Sally's toothbrush?" he said.

"Well, Sally took my brush and now we've taken hers, so it's tit for tat," said the doll. "Anyway, she never used her toothbrush! We wouldn't have taken it if she did."

I'm just wondering what is going to happen when Sally's mother discovers that Sally's toothbrush is gone. It's going to be very difficult for naughty little Sally to make her mother believe that she is cleaning her teeth each night with a toothbrush that isn't there!

POOR LITTLE BEAR

The monkey's got a lovely tail,
It swings him on his way,
The dog has such a happy one,
It wags itself all day.
The rocking horse's tail is fine,
It hangs down to the ground,
And oh, I love the kangaroo's,
It helps him jump around!
The clockwork mouse has got a tail,
The toy cat has one too,
And every animal, I'm sure,
That lives at London Zoo.
But I'm a Teddy Bear, and look,
I've no tail on behind!
Mine's been forgotten and I think
It's really most unkind!

Tiny and the Teddy Bear

One day Tiny took her teddy bear into the garden and played with him there. But when she went indoors at night, she forgot him.

In the middle of the night she awoke – and she remembered that she had left Teddy in the garden.

"Oh dear!" she said. "I'm too frightened to come and get you, Teddy. I am really."

But then she thought that Teddy must be feeling much more frightened, and it really wasn't his fault. So Tiny got out of bed, put on a coat, and went out into the garden. She did feel frightened, but she tried to be brave.

She found Teddy and picked him up. And then something sang from a bush nearby! It was such a very beautiful song that Tiny had to stay and listen.

"It must be a fairy, telling me not to be frightened!" she said, and she was glad. But it wasn't a fairy. It was a nightingale. Wasn't Tiny lucky to hear it?

THE ANGRY TOYS

Mary was unkind to her toys. She slapped the teddy bear, and stood her doll in the corner. She trod on her wooden soldiers and broke one.

They were very angry about it. One day they made up their minds to give Mary a fright. They waited until she was alone in the nursery, and then they all came alive!

The teddy bear walked up to Mary and slapped her hard. The doll pinched her leg. The wooden soldiers pricked her with their swords.

"Oh!" cried Mary. "Don't! What are you doing? Are you alive?"

"Yes," said the doll, "and we are treating you as you treated us. Do you like it?

"Not a bit," said Mary and she began to cry. "You are horrid toys."

"No, we are not," said the bear. "We are very nice toys. Go into the corner until you are sorry you said such an unkind thing."

Poor Mary had to stand in the corner just as she had made her toys do so often . She soon began to feel sorry.

"I'm very sorry I have been unkind to you, toys," she said. "I will never slap you or pinch you or tread on you again. I will be kind and love you."

"Well, we will love you too," said the toys, climbing on to Mary's knee.

"Listen!" said the bear. "Someone's coming. We must not be alive any more!" They all ran back to the toy cupboard and lay quite still: the teddy bear, the doll and the wooden soldiers.

And of course, Mary was never unkind to her toys again, but did her best to love and take care of them.

What I'm Going To Do

I'm going to ride a circus-horse,
And stand up on its back;
I'll have a whip in my right hand,
And won't I make it crack!

I'm going to keep a sweet-shop, too,
And weigh out sweets all day;
And when I think I'd like a few,
There'll be no need to pay!

I'm going to keep an aeroplane,
And p'raps a submarine,
And drive a monster motorcar
All painted red and green.

And then one day I'm going to join
Red Indians, brave and tall,
And wear big feathers round my head –
I'll like that best of all.

And oh! there's lots of other things
I've planned that I will do;
And when I'm quite grown up at last,
I do hope they'll come true!

TINY'S CIRCUS

Once Tiny went to the circus. When she saw how well the circus-folk rode their beautiful horses, and how they cantered round and round the ring, she wanted a circus of her own.

So you can see what she has done! She has made herself a ring of grass out in the orchard, and now she is a circus-girl, riding Teeny, her little Shetland pony! Round and round the ring she goes, just as she saw the people doing at the circus.

"Hup!" she says, "Hup, Teeny!" And Teeny tries to stand on her hind legs.

All Tiny's dolls and teddies are the people watching Tiny's circus. The fat teddy bear would so love to have a ride on the pony.

"It's your turn next, Teddy!" calls Tiny. "Well, toys, how do you like my circus? Do you think I ride well?"

And I wouldn't be a bit surprised if all the toys clapped and cheered as loudly as they could, would you?

I Shall Run Away!

It was nearly Christmas, and the toys had been asking one another what each of them wanted. "Would you like a new blue bow, Teddy?" said Angela the doll.

"How about some of your favourite iced buns?" the pink cat asked the toy dog.

"Would you like a little tiny knocker for the front door of your Ark?" the sailor doll asked Noah. He was very good at carving things out of wood, and he felt sure he could make a fine knocker.

But nobody asked the sailor doll what he would like. He knew what he wanted – a new blue bow for his jacket, new laces for his shoes, and a little pin for his hat.

"And nobody has asked me once what I'd like!" thought the sailor doll, gloomily. "It's too bad. Don't they like me? I know what I'll do. I'll ask Clockwork Mouse what he would like – and he is sure to say, 'And now, Sailor, tell me what you would like!'"

So the sailor doll asked the mouse – but all he said was, "Oh, please, I'd like two new whiskers!" He didn't ask the sailor doll what he wanted.

"That proves it!" said the sailor doll, miserably. "They don't like me. They're not going to give me any presents. Yet they've all told me what they want. Well – I'll give them the presents they want – but I shall run away just before Christmas! That will make them very, very sorry."

The toys couldn't think why Sailor Doll looked so gloomy. They got a bit tired of his miserable face after a while, and took no notice of him. That made him feel worse than ever! Just before Christmas the sailor doll decided to run away. "They'll be glad to have Christmas without me!" he thought. " Now – I want a little bag to pack my things in. Where is there one?"

He remembered seeing a little suitcase at the toy cupboard (a tiny little suitcase). He found it at last and took it over to a corner to pack his few things in it. "It feels a bit heavy," said Sailor, surprised. "I hope there's nothing in it."

He opened it – and out tumbled a whole lot of tiny parcels, all gaily done up in bits of Christmassy paper and tied with pretty string. Each one had a label. Sailor read them, and his cheeks blushed pink. "To Sailor with love", "For dear Sailor from the Clockwork Mouse", "For the nicest Sailor Doll in the world from Angela."

Sailor put everything back quickly into the little suitcase. Why – these were all presents hidden away by the toys, that they were going to give him at Christmas! They looked so exciting. How very kind of the toys. Sailor almost burst into tears.

"I'm so ashamed of myself," he said. "To think I got this suitcase to run away with – and it's the one the toys have hidden all the lovely presents in that they've made me for Christmas. I'm bad. I'm mean! I don't deserve any presents at all!"

He put the suitcase back. He felt so happy. The toys liked him after all! He was their "dear Sailor." Fancy that! Well, it just showed how silly it was to think people didn't like you. He worked hard at his presents for the others , making them as nicely as he could. He joked and smiled and was so very different that all the toys were surprised.

"He's a real dear," they said. "What a good thing we've got all the things he wants for Christmas. We didn't need to ask him, because we knew. How he'll love his new bow and hat pin and shoelaces and everything!"

He will, of course – but he shivers when he remembers how he nearly ran away!

PARTY AFTERNOON

I'm going to a party
This very afternoon,
I *do* wish four o'clock would come,
Soon, soon, soon!
I've got my frilly frock on,
And a sash that's silky blue,
I'm wearing silver sandals,
And my party necklace too.
I'm only Ann Belinda
As anyone can guess,
But I'm going to a party,
And I feel a real princess!

THE ANGRY TOYS

"Eileen!" said Mummy, "I want you to look through your toy cupboard and see what toys you can give away to the children in the hospital this Christmas, and to the orphanage."

"Oh, Mummy – I can't bear to give any of my toys away," said Eileen.

"Don't be selfish," said Mummy. "You have more toys than any other child in this town! Why, your cupboard is so full that they tumble out when you open the door!"

It was true that Eileen had a great many toys. She was lucky because she had seven uncles and five aunts, and they all gave her presents. She went to her toy cupboard and opened the door. A box of bricks fell out and a little toy dog.

"I can't give my nice toys away," said Eileen. "I won't give my big dolls away – or even my little dolls. I won't give away my little dolls' house, even though I have a much bigger one now. I like having two."

She looked at all her toy animals. She had so many! Some of them she hadn't even given a name to, and she didn't really love any of them.

"I don't want to give away any of my large family of animals," she thought. "They wouldn't like to be given away. They like to be together. Well – I really don't know what I can give."

At last she put a broken doll's chair and two torn books on one side to give away. That was all. Then it was time to go to bed.

When the house was quiet, the toys spoke to one another. "Did you ever know such a selfish child? Here we are, lots and lots of us, far too many for her to play with – and yet all she thinks she can spare is a broken chair and two spoilt books."

"I don't like belonging to a little girl like that," said the teddy bear. "I always wished I could belong to a nice kind little girl, who would let other children play with me sometimes. But Eileen is very selfish – she hides all her best toys when other boys and girls come to tea."

"I think she loves me and the old monkey best of all," said a big curly-haired doll, with a sweet smile and merry blue eyes. "But we don't love her, though we would like to. How can we love a little girl like that?"

"I'm not going to stay with her," said the teddy bear, suddenly. "I'm not! I know a poor little girl who would really love me. I shall go and live with her."

"And I won't stay either," said the clown. "I shall walk to the hospital, where lots of little ill children are. How they will love me! I won't stay with Eileen."

"I shall go to the hospital too," said the big rocking horse, suddenly. " I know the children who are just getting well again would like to have a ride on me."

"Let's all go," said the big doll. "Why should we stay with a little girl who isn't even generous enough to give one of her many toy animals away – why, she doesn't even know half of them! There's a toy dog at the back of the cupboard that she hasn't played with since she was given him."

"Let's go now," said the bear. So they all marched quietly out of the nursery, out of the garden door, and into the garden. Even the skittles went too.

36

First they went to the hospital. They had to wait till a nurse opened a door and came out — then half the toys slipped in! It was dark and quiet. They hurried into a great big room where many little children were asleep. There was a nurse at the far end of the big room, reading. She didn't see them at all. The rocking horse stood behind a screen. The other toys sat down or lay down.

"We will wait till morning," they said. Those toys that had not gone into the hospital made their way down to the orphanage. They slipped inside and hurried off to different rooms to find new owners. Soon they had all found new homes.

How pleased and surprised the nurses in the hospital were when they suddenly found all the lovely toys! "How did they get here?" they cried. "Oh, how glad the children will be to see them!"

The children in the orphanage were delighted too to wake up and find a furry rabbit or doll or toy dog cuddled up to them. They had so few toys that one nice one seemed wonderful to them.

Eileen went into her nursery the next morning and stopped to stare round in great surprise. Where were her toys? Only her books were there, and some bricks, and one or two other little things. No dolls, no teddy bear or clown, no toy animals or skittles – wherever had they all gone?

"Mummy! Mummy! My toys aren't here!" cried Eileen. "What have you done with them?"

"Nothing," said Mummy, in surprise. "Well – how strange that they've all gone!"

"But where have they gone?" said Eileen, beginning to cry. "Oh, Mummy – even my curly-haired doll and my old monkey, that I really did love, have gone!"

"They must have walked out by themselves," said Mummy, looking grave. "I expect they were disgusted with you when you wouldn't spare any of them to give away this Christmas. You knew you would have lots of new presents. You could easily have given a few away to children who have none."

"But where have they gone?" sobbed Eileen. "I want them to come back."

But they didn't come back. They are happy at the hospital, and in the orphanage, because they are really loved there. Eileen still can't think where they all went to.

So if you know her, you can tell her. Won't she be surprised?